The Honest Neighbors

retold by Barbara Spilman Lawson
illustrated by Esther Baran

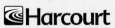

Harcourt

Orlando   Boston   Dallas   Chicago   San Diego

Visit *The Learning Site!*

www.harcourtschool.com

Long ago in a small village in China, five neighbors gathered at the public well to draw buckets of water for their daily needs. These neighbors had lived in the village their whole lives. The eldest was Chang, the jade carver. Next was Ming, a fisher. Wong was a baker and Woo, a farmer. The youngest was Lin, a silk maker.

As they drew their water, they chatted about the week's events. Ming declared that he had never caught so many fish as he had the day before. Wong said the bread he had baked that week was the tastiest ever. Woo said his cows had given more milk than any cows had ever given. Lin said the silk she had made was the softest in the world.

Chang, the eldest, shook his white head indignantly and said, "Such claims! Are we to believe such things? Yet I must admit that the jade that I am carving now is so beautiful that the emperor himself would pay twenty gold pieces to own it!"

The neighbors put their hands on their hips and scowled at Chang.

"I am truthful!" said Ming.

"I do not lie!" said Woo.

"I can be trusted!" said Wong.

"I am honest!" said Lin.

"Are we all honorable?" asked Chang. "How are we to know?"

Chang sat down on the stone well. "I recall the time when the emperor traveled from his palace to a city far away. He passed through our little village, and the horses drawing his carriage were frightened by a wild dog. The horses bolted. The carriage shook so much that the emperor's purse was thrown out the carriage window."

"I remember," said Ming. "Gold coins rolled all over the village and into the countryside. My wife was elated, for she believed we could keep the ones we found by the river. However, I told her they did not belong to us, and we gave them back to the emperor."

"Indeed?" asked Wong. "How did you buy your new boat if you did not keep the gold? I myself found some of the emperor's gold on the doorstep of my bakery. At first, I thought it to be just golden spots of sunlight. After a closer look, I saw it was gold."

"You kept it to pay the stone maker to build your new oven," said Woo, spitefully.

"No," said Wong. "It was my privilege to return the gold coins to the emperor. The emperor thanked me and said I am valuable to the whole of China, for I am trustworthy and honest."

Woo shook his head. "I do not believe you, neighbor," he said. "I found some of the emperor's gold coins. They had rolled down the road and into my fields of rice. As I was bending down, pulling grain from the water, my fingers touched the smooth, round pieces."

"You used them to get new rakes," said Lin.

"No," said Woo. "At first, I thought I had grown precious metal. When I looked closely, however, I saw the emperor's face stamped on each coin. Right away, I knew they could not belong to me. I hastened to the village, where the emperor's carriage still waited, and returned every last piece. The emperor was glad."

"You did not keep a single coin?" asked Lin. "Not a one?"

"No," said Woo. "I do not keep what is not mine."

"I recall that day," said Lin. "I was in my silkworm garden, preparing to collect the precious threads to weave into fabric. Suddenly, I heard sharp pings on the stone walkway. I turned to see a handful of gold coins rolling my way. I wondered if they were a payment from a passing customer who was in too much of a hurry to stop and say hello. When I saw the emperor's face on the coins, I knew they were not for me. I collected them and took them to the emperor, who was grateful."

Chang rubbed his chin. "I wonder, did you keep some to buy your new loom?" he asked.

Lin shook her head angrily.

Chang said, "I heard the emperor's carriage rumbling through the village and peered out of my shop to see the sight. I saw the wild dog jump from the shadows and snap at the horses. I saw the horses bolt and the carriage shake. I saw the emperor's purse fly like a bird through his open window and gold coins scatter like leaves in autumn."

"You collected some yourself, did you not?" asked Woo. "You bought a set of new jade-carving tools. I have seen them."

"I did not," said Chang. "Gold coins did roll into my shop and land at the feet of a lovely green statue I was carving. Oh, it would have been tempting for a shiftless person to hide the coins away and never tell anyone. However, I scooped them up and raced outside as fast as my tired old legs could carry me. The carriage was rumbling up the street, enveloped in a cloud of dust. I called out to the driver to wait. He pulled at the reins, and the horses stopped. Humbly, I bowed to the emperor and gave him what was his. The emperor offered me a coin as a reward, but I told him, 'No, these are yours, not mine, oh Great Emperor.'"

The neighbors all began to argue and shout, declaring their own honesty and the dishonesty of the others. They did not notice a cart pulling up next to the well. A well-dressed man got out of it.

"Hello, there," said the man. The neighbors stopped arguing and turned toward the stranger.

"Who are you?" asked Wong.

"I'm just passing by," said the man, "on my way to see the emperor. I have a gift for him." He nodded at his cart. It was covered with a red velvet curtain at its back.

"What luxury could be back there?" wondered Lin aloud.

"I am a goldsmith," said the man. "My talents are known throughout China. The emperor heard of my skills and ordered a special bell for the palace."

"A bell?" said Woo. "How special is a bell?"

"This bell is made of pure gold," said the goldsmith. "It shines like the sun. Its sound is clear and perfect."

"Still, it is just a bell," said Lin.

"Ah," said the goldsmith. "You are wrong, my friend. The bell can tell whether or not someone is telling the truth."

The neighbors' eyes lit up. Now they could find out which of them was truthful.

"I heard you arguing when I arrived at the well," said the wise goldsmith. "It seems you do not believe each other when you say you returned gold pieces to the emperor. I challenge each of you to put your hand behind the curtain and touch the bell. If the bell remains silent, you have told the truth. If someone who is not truthful touches the bell, it rings so loudly that everyone in the empire can hear it."

The neighbors looked at each other.

"Do you accept my challenge?" asked the goldsmith. "Who will go first?"

Chang nodded his assent. He stepped up to the velvet curtain and put his hand behind it. A moment later, he removed his hand and said, "It did not ring when I touched it. This proves I am telling the truth."

Ming pushed his way to the cart and slipped his hand behind the curtain. Again, there was no sound from the bell. He took his hand out and smiled. "I do not lie," he said. "Who is next?"

Wong wiped his hands on his apron and approached the cart. He put his hand behind the red curtain to touch the bell. Again, there was no ring. He laughed and declared, "Now you know me to be a man of truth!"

Woo was next. He cleared his throat and slowly
slipped his hand behind the velvet curtain.
Everyone leaned forward to listen. There was no
sound from the bell. Woo withdrew his hand and
said, "You see? I bought my new rakes with honest
money, earned with my hard labor and efforts! I do
not need to steal!"

Lin looked at the others and then walked up to
the cart. The others began to whisper among
themselves, certain that Lin would be found out as
a thief. Lin placed her hand behind the red velvet
curtain. The bell did not ring.

The neighbors stared at each other, stunned.

"We are all honest folk!" declared Woo.

The wise goldsmith said, "We are not finished." Then he asked them all to hold out their hands. Ming, Wong, Woo, and Lin all had golden dust on the hand that had touched the bell. Chang's hand, however, was clean.

"You did not tell the truth," said the wise goldsmith, "and so you did not dare touch the bell."

Shamefacedly, Chang began to ad lib excuses for keeping the emperor's gold. The goldsmith did not wait to listen. He climbed into his cart and drove off.

The neighbors looked at Chang and shook their heads. They collected their buckets of water to return home.

"Wait," said Chang. "I am glad to know my neighbors are honest. I want to be honest, too."

."The gold you kept is long gone," said Lin. "You bought tools for carving jade."

"Then I shall take my finest statue to the emperor," said Chang. "It is of greater value than the coins I kept. Perhaps doing so will restore my honor, with both the emperor and with you. From now on, I will always be honest."

The neighbors nodded. Chang went home and packed the statue for the long journey ahead.